Amadito and the Hero Children

Amadito y los Niños Héroes

UNIVERSITY OF NEW MEXICO PRESS   ALBUQUERQUE

...to and the Hero Children

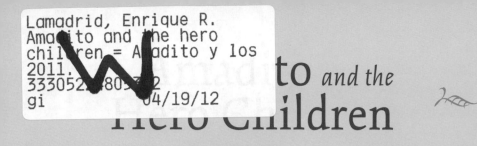

Amadito y los Niños Héroes

Enrique R. Lamadrid

Illustrations by **Amy Córdova**   Afterword by **Michael León Trujillo**

For Yasmín

Printed and bound in China by Everbest Printing Company, Ltd.
through Four Colour Imports, Ltd. | Production location: Guangdong, China
Date of Production: June 2011 | Cohort: Batch I

16 15 14 13 12 11   1 2 3 4 5 6

Library of Congress Cataloging-in-Publication Data

Lamadrid, Enrique R.
Amadito and the hero children = Amadito y los niños héroes / Enrique Lamadrid ;
foreword by Genaro M. Padilla ; afterword by Michael León Trujillo ; illustrations
by Amy Córdova.
     p. cm. — (Pasó por aquí series on the Nuevomexicano literary heritage)
Parallel title: Amadito y los niños héroes
Includes bibliographical references.
Summary: A brief fictional recounting of legendary epidemics that struck the American
Southwest—the smallpox epidemics of the eighteenth and nineteenth centuries and the
influenza epidemic during World War I—which ravaged many rural communities throughout
the West. Includes author's notes about the characters.
ISBN 978-0-8263-4979-8 (cloth : alk. paper) — ISBN 978-0-8263-4980-4 (electronic)
[1. Epidemics—Fiction. 2. Southwest, New—History—Fiction. 3. Mexican Americans—
Fiction. 4. Spanish language materials—Bilingual.] I. Córdova, Amy, ill. II. Title.
  PZ73.L2777 2011
  [Fic]—dc22
                                        2011009197

Design and composition: Melissa Tandysh | Text composed in Minister Std

Pasó por Aquí
Series on the Nuevomexicano
Literary Heritage
Edited by Genaro M. Padilla,
Enrique R. Lamadrid, &
A. Gabriel Meléndez

NOTE FROM THE SERIES EDITORS

WE AT PASÓ POR AQUÍ ARE PLEASED TO OFFER Enrique R. Lamadrid's rousing bilingual story, *Amadito and the Hero Children / Amadito y los Niños Héroes*, a fact-based fiction about a Nuevo Mexicano village's fight against two deadly epidemics that doomed thousands of people in the Hispano Southwest: smallpox and influenza. Separated in time by more than a century, both nine-year-old protagonists are from the village of Chamisal, tucked high in a valley of the Sangre de Cristo Mountains. Like a little pilgrim, María Peregrina arrives in 1810 as a carrier of the precious smallpox vaccine. True to his name, Amadito proves his love for family and community in the midst of the deadly flu pandemic in 1918. Like so many traditional Nuevo Mexicano *cuentos*, this is a story of hope in which children are intrepid, brave, and smart enough to overcome major obstacles against huge odds.

Professor Lamadrid's expertise as a folklorist provides a broad cultural, literary, and historical context to offer contemporary audiences, especially schoolchildren, an inspirational tale for their own challenges in an often-troubling world. One of the challenges that Nuevo Mexicano children face is the recovery of their linguistic heritage—the Spanish language. Together with Professor Michael León Trujillo's learned and illuminating afterword, this modern day cuento can be taught by teachers and parents in New Mexico and beyond who wish to help children understand their role in confronting worldwide threats to our common well-being, like pandemic disease or the ominous results of global warming. Rather than passively hoping all turns out well in the end, *Amadito and the Hero Children* will help young readers imagine themselves as capable of similar acts of heroism, to help them build confidence to grow into adult heroes who put their education, determination, and ethical vision to the service of building a truly cooperative and coherent world, locally and globally.

For the Pasó Por Aquí Editors,
Genaro M. Padilla
University of California, Berkeley

ACKNOWLEDGMENTS | AGRADECIMIENTOS

DEBTS OF GRATITUDE AND APPRECIATION:
To the *Resolaneros* of the Academia de la Nueva Raza of Embudo, New Mexico—Tomás Atencio and Consuelo Pacheco for their constant concern for *La vida buena y sana*, Estevan Arellano for his encouragement, E. A. "Tony" Mares for his poetic advice, and Alejandro López for sharing the taped interviews from the amazing Academia oral history project of 1971–1972. Many of the stories about *remedios* and memories of the influenza pandemic of 1918 recorded there confirmed what I found in my own interviews in the Española valley and with Dr. José Amado Domínguez conducted in the 1980s. To my grandson, Inti Martín Lamadrid Ortiz, the great-great-grandson of Mamá Virginia and Papá José Inés. To the members and healers of this extended family, including Amadito himself; Dr. John DeFlice; Gianna DeFlice, L.Ac., MSOM; and Ana Yasmín Lamadrid, R.N. To *prima* Barbara MacPherson for her colorful childhood memories of Chamisal. To my *compadre* Charles Briggs and Clara Mantini for their heroic medical and political leadership in the cholera and rabies epidemics in the Orinoco delta. To Rudolfo Anaya who introduced me to the world of children's books. To Amy Córdova for bringing this story alive in her art. To Eleuterio Santiago Díaz for keeping wise vigil over the bilingual texts. To Robert O. Valdez, director of the UNM Robert Wood Johnson Center for Health Policy, for sharing his research on Dr. Xavier Balmis's 1803 Expedición Real Filantrópica de la Vacuna and on smallpox epidemics in New Mexico. To New Mexico State Representative Lorenzo "Larry" Larrañaga and the descendents of Dr. Cristóval Larrañaga. And to "Cuernoblanco," Clark Whitehorn, editor-in-chief of UNM Press and his editorial team for believing in this book.

Down from La Jicarita, that majestic mountain with the little gourd name, a canyon filled with ponderosa pines broadens into a slender valley filled with chamisa brush to the town of Chamisal, down to the Domínguez family ranch and its fields of beans and more beans. In early fall, especially in the years of the First World War when the young men were fighting in France, every available child was recruited to pick the pods. Bushels upon bushels were spread out in the sun to dry for a week before *la trilla*. For the threshing, other villages ran goats round and round the packed-earth threshing floor to loosen the pinto beans from the pods.

Bajando La Jicarita, esa montaña majestuosa con su nombre tan chiquito, hay un cañón lleno de pinabetes que se abre a un vallecito estrecho lleno de chamizos hasta la placita de Chamisal, bajando hacia el ranchito de la familia Domínguez con sus campos de frijoles y más frijoles. Comenzando el otoño, especialmente en los años de la Primera Guerra Mundial cuando los jóvenes peleaban en Francia, todos los niños del valle se juntaban para pepenar los frijoles. Fanegas y más fanegas se apilaban en el sol para secarse una semana antes de la trilla. En otras placitas la gente corría cabras sobre las eras para que soltaran los frijoles de sus vainas.

In Chamisal, the Domínguez kids were in charge. At ten, Anita was the oldest, followed by José Amado, Enrique, Isaac, and Pablita. Only two-year-old Fermilia had to stay home with Mamá Virginia while the other children raked the beans onto big canvas tarps and jumped up and down, singing every song they knew, and this one especially for the occasion:

> *Frijolitos pintos,*   Little pinto beans,
> *claveles morados,*   purple carnations,
> *¡ay, cómo sufren*   oh, how they suffer,
> *los enamorados!*   those who are in love!

Only the oldest boy, José Amado, paused to think about the words of the silly little song. For his nine years, Amadito was more thoughtful and serious than other children his age. The *frijolitos pintos* were obvious, for he was standing at the edge of a bean field.

"But why is love painful? And what are the purple *claveles* for?" he asked big sister Anita. Amadito had only seen them at weddings and funerals, especially the paper ones.

Everybody always laughed at the next verse. It was funny and disturbing at the same time:

En Chamisal, los muchitos de la familia Domínguez se encargaban de todo. Con sus diez años Anita era la hermana mayor, seguida por José Amado, Enrique, Isaac y Pablita. Solamente Fermilia, con sus dos años, se quedaba en casa con Mamá Virginia mientras los otros muchitos sacaban los grandes cotencios, echaban los frijoles encima y brincaban sobre ellos, cantando todas las canciones que sabían, y en particular, esta para la ocasión:

> *Frijolitos pintos,*
> *claveles morados,*
> *¡ay, cómo sufren*
> *los enamorados!*

Solamente el hermano mayor, José Amado, se detenía a pensar en la cancioncita tan tonta. Para sus nueve veranos, Amadito era más inquisitivo y serio que los otros niños de su edad. Los "frijolitos pintos" eran obvios para él, porque estaba parado en la orilla de un campo de frijoles.

"¿Pero por qué duele el amor? ¿Y para qué sirven los 'claveles morados'?" le preguntaba a su hermana Anita. Amadito sólo los había visto en los casorios y los funerales, especialmente los de papel.

Todo el mundo se reía de los siguientes versos. Eran chistosos y curiosos a la vez:

Primero da viruela,
luego sarampión,
le quedó la cara
como un chicharrón.

First smallpox strikes,
then the measles,
his/her face was left
like a pork crackling.

The other kids laughed about having a face like a *chicharrón*. Who would fall in love with you if you had a scarred and ugly face? But what was *viruela*, the smallpox? Amadito knew about *sarampión*, because he, his brothers, and his sisters had had measles and then chicken pox one right after the other. His mother told him that smallpox was a deadly disease that not that long ago would come to ravage New Mexico every ten years or so.

"*Como la mano negra* . . . like the black hand of Death," she told him, "la viruela took away many, many children and old people with great pain and suffering." It reached into even the most remote and protected valleys of the Sierra de la Sangre de Cristo. Then came *la vacuna*, the vaccine, and finally people were safe. Amadito knew it had something to do with the smooth, round scar on his arm. He tapped it gently with his finger as his mother spoke.

Primero da viruela,
luego sarampión,
le quedó la cara
como un chicharrón.

Los otros muchitos se reían de la idea de tener una cara achicharronada. ¿Quién se enamoraría de ti si tuvieras una cara fea y cicatrizada? Pero ¿qué era la viruela? Amadito sabía del sarampión porque él y sus hermanos y hermanas lo tuvieron y después la varicela uno tras otro. Su mamá le había dicho que la viruela era un mal muy peligroso que no hacía tanto tiempo venía a Nuevo México cada diez años o algo así.

"Como la mano negra de la Muerte," le dijo, "la viruela se llevaba muchos, muchos niños y gente grande con gran dolor y sufrimiento." Penetraba los valles más remotos y protegidos de la Sierra de la Sangre de Cristo. Entonces llegó la vacuna, y por fin la gente quedó a salvo. Amadito sabía que la vacuna tenía algo que ver con la cicatriz redonda y lisa en su brazo. La tocaba ligeramente con el dedo mientras su madre hablaba.

For two whole days a stiff wind blew through the beautiful October days. The kids worked hard, tossing armfuls of crushed pods into the air as the wind blew all the dry husks away. The kids then scooped the beans into fifty-pound *guangoche* sacks and loaded them into the family buckboard wagon for the trip to Embudo Station. Papá José Inés was going to take Amadito with him to sell the beans and bring back supplies for the family store. It would be the last summer adventure before school began!

School was a family affair in Chamisal. Mamá Virginia was the teacher. Her father had sent her to Normal School in Grand Junction, Colorado, for a year of teacher training. Now she taught many of the kids of Chamisal, even though there was no school building there yet. It was easier to teach at home than to pack her kids over the hill every day to the nuns in Peñasco or to the boarding school in Chimayó. She kept her math lessons in a ledger book and used the stories of *One Thousand and One Nights*, two McGuffey Readers, her Spanish Bible, and the weekly copies of a newspaper, *La Revista de Taos*, for reading lessons. The news was worrying Mamá a lot lately.

"*Gracias a Dios*, the Great War is ending," she read aloud from the paper to the family at the table one morning. "But our boys are still dying!"

Por dos días enteros un viento recio sopló en los hermosos días de octubre. Los muchitos trabajaban duro, tirando brazadas de vainas pisadas para arriba mientras el viento se llevaba la hojarasca. Entonces echaban los frijoles en guangoches de cincuenta libras para cargarlos en el carro de bestias y llevarlos a la Estación de Embudo. Papá José Inés llevaría a Amadito con él para vender los frijoles y traer mercancía para la tiendita de la familia. ¡Sería la última aventura del verano antes del comienzo de la escuela!

La escuela era un asunto de familia en Chamisal. Mamá Virginia era la maestra. Su papá le había mandado de a la Escuela Normal en Grand Junction, Colorado, para ser maestra. Ahora enseñaba a muchos de los niños de Chamisal, aunque no había un edificio escolar todavía. Era más fácil enseñar en casa que mandar a los hijos a diario donde las monjas de Peñasco al otro lado del cerro o a la escuela de internos de Chimayó. Guardaba sus lecciones de matemática en un cuaderno de negocios y para enseñar lectura y escritura usaba los cuentos de las *Mil y una noches*, dos libros americanos de McGuffey, su Biblia en español y las copias del periódico semanal, *La Revista de Taos*. Las noticias le preocupaban mucho a Mamá últimamente.

"Gracias a Dios, se termina la Gran Guerra," le leyó del papel en voz alta a la familia en la mesa una mañana. "¡Pero nuestros jóvenes siguen muriendo!"

The obituaries read that four soldiers from Taos and Río Arriba counties had died in France, not from German shells, but from *la influeza española*. They called it "Spanish flu," not because it was Spanish, but because the only newspapers that reported it were in Spain, a neutral country in the war. Even though tens of thousands were dying, French and British papers made no mention of the epidemic. The push to win the war would not be sidetracked.

The flu started just like a *resfriado*, with chills, sore throat, sniffles, fever, and cough. But unlike a common cold, it quickly got worse. Much worse. By the second day, the sick person could no longer stand up because of the bone-cracking pain. If he or she could not find a place to rest and lie down, death could come soon. Part of the cure was to stay home near your own bed and to keep away from others. It was best to not sit or stand, but to stay horizontal. Even with proper care and plenty of warm liquids, many people died within a week from *pulmonía* and complications. The suffocating pneumonia made lips and faces turn blue, and the victim would slip into a deep coma from which many never awoke.

En los obituarios se anunciaba que cuatro soldados de los condados de Taos y Río Arriba habían muerto en Francia, no por los proyectiles alemanes sino de la influenza española. La llamaban así, no porque fuera española, sino porque los únicos periódicos que reportaban sobre ella eran los de España, un país neutral en la guerra. Aunque millares de personas estaban muriendo, los periódicos de Francia e Inglaterra no mencionaron la epidemia. El proyecto de ganar la guerra no iba a ser desviado.

La influenza lo mismo como un resfriado, empezaba con escalofríos, dolor de garganta, moqueos, fiebre y tos. Pero a diferencia del resfrío común, pronto se hacía peor. Mucho peor. Para el segundo día, el enfermo ya no podía pararse por los dolores en huesos. Si él o ella no encontraba un lugar para acostarse y descansar, se podría morir pronto. Parte del remedio era quedarse en casa junto a la cama, alejado de los demás. Era mejor no sentarse ni pararse, sino permanecer recostado. Aun con mucho cuidado y muchos líquidos calientes, mucha gente se moría dentro de una semana de la pulmonía y sus complicaciones. La gente se sofocaba; los labios y la cara se les volvían azules. La víctima caía en una coma profunda de la que muchos no despertaban.

A week later, Amadito read from an article from *La Revista* to the family.

"Look, *la influencia* has come to Albuquerque, Santa Fe, and Taos." He saw where Mamá had underlined the headlines: "Black Hand of Death Reaches in from Europe. New Mexico Suffers with the World."

There was no cure, no sanctuary, and no remedy for what the people called "la influencia" in local Spanish, not the original Italian name. The epidemic was about to "influence" their lives forever. Only the *oshá*—wild celery root—seemed to give any relief to the sore throat. Many folks believed that the juice of the *cebolla morada*—the purple onion—would help. Maybe because the color matched the lips of the afflicted? After baking it in the oven, you mash it with *piloncillo*—those raw sugar cones—to make a thick syrup. Mamá Virginia had asked her husband to order a box of cebollas moradas to be shipped to them on the train with the other goods from Española, just in case.

"We'll bring you two boxes!" Papá laughed. "Plus that round mirror and frame that you wanted!"

Una semana más tarde, Amadito le leyó a la familia de un artículo de *La Revista*.

"Mira, 'la influencia' ha llegado a Albuquerque, Santa Fe y Taos." Vio donde Mamá había subrayado los titulares: "La Mano Negra de la Muerte nos Llega de Europa. Nuevo México Sufre con el Mundo."

No había ni cura, ni refugio, ni remedio para lo que la gente llamaba "la influencia" en español local en vez de usar el nombre original del italiano. La epidemia iba a "influenciar" sus vidas para siempre. Solamente la raíz del oshá o apio silvestre aliviaba el dolor de garganta. Mucha gente creía que el jugo de la cebolla morada ayudaba. Quizás era porque tenía el mismo color que los labios de los enfermos. Después de cocerlas en el horno, se machucan con el piloncillo para hacer un jarabe espeso. Por si acaso, Mamá Virginia le había pedido a su esposo que trajera una caja de cebolla morada con los otros abarrotes que venían en el tren de Española.

"¡Te traeremos dos cajas!" se reía Papá. "¡Y ese espejo redondo que querías!"

The next day Amadito hitched the mules to the wagon for the trip down to Embudo. They tossed their heads happily in anticipation. Papá José Inés paid special attention to the wagon's brakes, since the winding road was very steep and rocky. He always whistled merrily to himself on trips. They left town before sunrise and rolled into what people were calling "Dixon Town," an upper Embudo village that an Americano postmaster had just named for himself. Things were unusually quiet.

"Papá?" Amadito questioned. "Where is everybody, why aren't people picking their apples yet?" He noticed the piles of ripe yellow and red fruit in yards and orchards beginning to rot on the ground. Papá stopped whistling.

"*¡Diosito de mi vida!*" He gasped when he saw that three houses had large bows tied from black cloth hanging on their doors. Amadito had never seen this kind of adornment, but he knew right away what it meant. They knocked at the door of their *primo* Jorge in a house just below the plaza. Instead of inviting them inside for coffee and lunch as he usually did, he met them nervously on the portal.

El próximo día Amadito enganchó las mulas al carro para el viaje a Embudo. Las mulas meneaban las cabezas, alegres de anticipación. Papá José Inés prestó mucha atención a los frenos, ya que el camino serpentino era muy empinado y pedregoso. Siempre chiflaba alegremente cuando viajaba. Salieron de la casa antes del amanecer y llegaron a "Dixon Town," la plaza de Embudo de arriba que un estafetero americano acababa de dar su propio nombre. Estaba todo demasiado tranquilo.

"¿Papá?" Amadito preguntó. "¿Dónde está toda la gente, por qué no están pepenando las manzanas?" Notó que habían pilas de fruta amarilla y colorada en los patios y arboledas que estaban empezando a podrirse. Papá dejó de chiflar.

"¡Diosito de mi vida!" susurró cuando vio que tres casas tenían grandes moños de tela negra en las puertas. Amadito nunca había visto este tipo de adorno, pero entendía de una vez lo que significaba. Tocaron a la puerta de su primo Jorge en una casa un poco más abajo de la plaza. En vez de invitarles a tomar café y comida como siempre, los recibió ansiosamente en el portal.

"*No entren, sigan. Estamos en cuarentena, que Dios los guarde.* Don't come in, go on. We are in quarantine, may God keep you."

The flu had already arrived on the train, the famous narrow-gauge "Chile Line" from Santa Fe and Española to San Antonito, Colorado. First a twelve-year-old child had died, and many mourners that had attended the *velorio*, or funeral wake, had now taken sick. No one realized how important it was to cover a cough or sneeze, or how the infection spread by touching your nose or eyes. And they had no idea how washing hands with soap could keep the disease away. They did realize that the influenza was contagious and spread by direct contact. So the *cuarentena* was called, and families were staying inside their houses. Armed men had gone down from Dixon to Embudo Station to discourage strangers from getting off the train and bringing in more illness. But it was already too late.

Papá José Inés and Amadito said good-bye to their primo Jorge and headed down past the last arroyo and through the little gorge of the Río Embudo to La Junta, the place where it flowed into the Río Grande. The converging canyons brought the flow of both rivers dashing together like in a funnel or, in Spanish, *embudo*.

"Papá?" Amadito asked. "Is Embudo named for the canyons or for those embudo-shaped hills by the river?" No answer.

"*No entren, sigan. Estamos en cuarentena, que Dios los guarde,*" les dijo.

La influenza ya había llegado en el tren, el famoso ferrocarril de vía estrecha "Chile Line" de Santa Fe y Española a San Antonito, Colorado. Primero murió un muchacho de doce años, y muchos dolientes que habían asistido al velorio se habían enfermado. Nadie sabía la importancia de cubrir la tos o el estornudo. No entendían que la infección se transmitía al tocarse la nariz o los ojos ni que se podía prevenir lavándose las manos con jabón. Sí comprendían que la influenza se contagiaba por contacto directo, así que se impuso la cuarentena, y las familias comenzaron a quedarse dentro de sus casas. Varios hombres armados se habían ido de Dixon a la Estación de Embudo para disuadir a los fuereños de que se bajaran del tren para impedir más contagio. Pero ya era demasiado tarde.

Papá José Inés y Amadito se despidieron del primo Jorge y pasaron el último arroyo por el pequeño desfiladero del Río Embudo a La Junta, el lugar donde desembocaba en el Río Grande. Los cañones juntaban el agua de los dos ríos que chocaban como en un embudo.

"¿Papá?" preguntó Amadito. "¿El Embudo recibió ese nombre por los cañones o por esos cerros que parecen embudos junto al río?" No recibió respuesta.

They traveled without a word and crossed the old wooden bridge to Embudo Station. Soon the steam whistle and puffing of the two o'clock train could be heard echoing off the black lava cliffs. It usually sounded cheerful, but today it sounded like a lament. They saw two men with rifles meet the train. The locomotive stopped to get water from the water tower and its redwood tank. Only a few people were on the train. None made a move to get down. The clerk waved from the freight car.

In a quick transaction, Papá José Inés collected his pay for six hundred pounds of pinto beans. Then he exchanged most of the cash to the clerk for the merchandise for the family store. Their livelihood for a good part of the year depended on this single transaction. Amadito helped with the checklist as their wagon was loaded:

Padre e hijo viajaron en silencio y cruzaron el viejo puente de tablas hacia la Estación de Embudo. Pronto oyeron el silbato y los resoplidos del tren de las dos de la tarde y los ecos por los precipicios de lava negra. Normalmente sonaba alegre, pero ese día era como un lamento. Vieron a dos hombres salir con rifles para recibir el tren. La locomotora paró para abastecerse de agua de la torre de agua y su tanque de madera de palo colorado. Muy poca gente había en el tren. Nadie intentó bajarse. El empleado les saludó desde el carro de carga.

En una rápida transacción, Papá José Inés tomó el pago por seiscientas libras de frijoles pintos. Luego devolvió la mayor parte del dinero al empleado para pagar por la mercancía de la tiendita de la familia. El sustento para la mayor parte del año dependía básicamente de este negocio. Amadito ayudó a cotejar con la lista mientras cargaban el carro de bestias:

Light for the darkness: a drum of kerosene for lamps, plus wicks, boxes of matches, and replacement glass globes.

Mamá Virginia's round mirror.

Household hardware: axes, shovels, hoes, saws, nails, skillets, pots.

Kitchen staples: Three large wooden boxes of piloncillo. A fifty-pound sack of coffee beans. Another of salt. Two cases of the small cans of baking soda the people called *salarata*. Spices like pepper, cloves, and cinnamon.

Food for travelers and shepherds: cases of cans of corned beef, potted meat, Vienna sausages, sardines, condensed milk, and that greatest of delicacies, deviled ham.

For spring gardens: A large envelope of fancy kitchen garden seeds—lettuce, turnips, radish, and more—that people were anxious to try out next spring. And a few bare-root fruit trees and lilacs to get into the ground as soon as possible.

For the kids: Boxes of lemon and cinnamon drops, black licorice, ribbon peppermint candy. The oranges for Christmas came later.

For sewing: Bolts of color print and black cotton cloth, muslin, and striped ticking. Wool cloth for coats. Needles and thread.

For the influenza: two crates of purple onions.

Luz para la oscuridad: un barril de querosén para las lámparas, mechas, cajas de fósforos y bombillas de vidrio.

El espejo redondo de Mamá Virginia.

Ferretería de casa: hachas, palas, cavadores, serruchos, clavos, puelas, cazuelas.

Comestibles para la cocina: Tres cajas grandes de piloncillo. Un saco de cincuenta libras de café en grano. Otro saco de sal. Dos cajas de botes de "salarata" para hornear. Especies como pimienta, clavos y canela.

Abarrotes para viajeros y pastores: cajas de botes de carne argentina, botes de puré de carne, salchichitas de Viena, sardinas, leche condensada y la mayor delicia de todas, el jamón del diablo.

Para los jardines de primavera: Un sobre grande de semillas finas—lechuga, nabos, rábanos y todo—lo que la gente estaba deseosa de probar la próxima primavera. Y para sembrar en seguida, ramitas de lila y arbolitos de fruta.

Para los niños: Cajas de dulces de limón y canela, anís negro, caramelo de listón de yerba buena. Las naranjas se conseguían más tarde, para la Navidad.

Para coser: Rollos de tela grabada y de tela negra de algodón, rollos de muselina blanca y rayada. Tela de lana para abrigos. Agujas y rollos de hilo.

Para la influenza: dos cajas de cebolla morada.

Instead of lingering at the station house to listen to the latest news, the father and son left as quickly as they had come and started back up the canyon. Since they couldn't stay at the house of their primo Jorge, they camped by the Río Grande in a grove of grandmother cottonwoods, with brilliant yellow leaves quaking in the breeze. Dinner was a whole can of corned beef with wheat tortillas they had brought from home.

Early the next morning they started back up the Río Embudo. As they approached Dixon, they were surprised to hear the sound of bells: the somber bell of San Antonio's Church and the high, clear bells of the Presbyterians across the street. The churches were empty, the plaza was empty, for funerals and gatherings had been cancelled and forbidden. All they saw were a few men in the *camposanto* and the fresh graves they had just dug. The only person out walking around was Inocencio, a street kid, who grinned and told them, *"Buen tiempo para morir; están enterrando gratis . . .* It's a good time to die; they are burying people for free."

They smiled but didn't laugh.

En vez de entretenerse en la estación para escuchar las últimas noticias, el padre y el hijo salieron tan rápido como habían llegado y subieron el cañón. Como no podían quedarse en casa del primo Jorge, acamparon al lado del Río Grande en una alameda de álamos gordos, con brillantes hojas doradas temblando en la brisa. La cena fue un bote entero de carne argentina con tortillas de trigo que habían traído de la casa.

Muy temprano la siguiente mañana subieron por el Río Embudo. Cuando se acercaban Dixon, les sorprendieron las campanas: la melancólica campana de la Iglesia de San Antonio y las campanas altas y claras de los presbiterianos al otro lado de la calle. Las iglesias estaban vacías, la plaza estaba vacía, porque los funerales y velorios habían sido cancelados y prohibidos. Sólo vieron algunos hombres en el camposanto y los sepulcros que acababan de excavar. La única persona que se paseaba era Inocencio, un joven de la calle. Les sonrió y les dijo, "Buen tiempo para morir, están enterrando gratis."

Ellos se sonrieron pero no se rieron.

As they headed up the canyon and the winding road towards Peñasco, the two mules looked over their shoulders towards the valley. They were still hoping to stop in Embudo to snack on fallen apples in the orchards. When the travelers reached the top of the *cuestecita*, they drank some water. Papá José Inés quickly gathered a few sticks, lit a small fire, and then cut a bunch of green cedar boughs. Amadito wondered why anyone would throw green cedar on a fire. A sudden billow of white smoke puffed up.

"Walk through the smoke three times, *mi'jito*."

"*Por qué*, Daddy, why?"

"*En el nombre del Padre, del Hijo, del Espíritu Santo.*"

The fragrant smoke gave special power to the familiar blessing. With tears in their eyes, they prayed for the health of their family. As they hurried through the little forest of ponderosa pines on the other side, a gust of wind brought the sound of more bells, this time from Río Lucío and Peñasco. Even though there was still a small chain of hills yet to cross, they even imagined they heard the bell of Chamisal.

What a relief it was when they saw Mamá Virginia and five brothers and sisters waiting on the long portal. *Gracias a Dios*, everyone was all right.

Mientras subían el cañón y el camino serpentino hacia Peñasco, las dos mulas miraban hacia atrás hacia el valle. Todavía tenían la esperanza de pararse en Embudo para comer de las manzanas caídas en las arboledas. Cuando los viajeros llegaron a la cuestecita, tomaron agua. Papá José Inés juntó unos palitos, prendió una lumbre y luego cortó unas ramitas de sabino. A Amadito no se le hubiera ocurrido echarle ramas verdes a la lumbre. Una nube repentina de humo blanco subió.

"Pasa tres veces por el humo, mi'jito."

"¿Por qué, *Daddy*, por qué?"

"En el nombre del Padre, del Hijo, del Espíritu Santo."

El humo fragante prestó un poder especial a la bendición familiar. Con lágrimas en los ojos, rezaron por la salud de su familia. Mientras se apuraban por el bosquecito de pinabetes al otro lado, una ráfaga de viento trajo el sonido de más campanas, esta vez de Río Lucío y Peñasco. Aunque todavía había una cordillera de cerritos para cruzar, creyeron oír la campana de Chamisal.

Qué alivio cuando vieron a Mamá Virginia y los cinco hermanos y hermanas esperando en el largo portal. Gracias a Dios, todos estaban bien.

Papá and Amadito unloaded the wagon. Right away, Anita and Mamá started making purple onion syrup in case anyone would need it. The boxes of onions were left on the portal so that if neighbors needed any, they wouldn't come inside. Hanging from the *viga* of the ceiling was a sack of fresh oshá. There was nothing to do but wait and pray the *rosario* in the evening.

Since not that much could be done for the influenza, Amadito felt grieved and frustrated. Now they could not go out to play or find their friends. Were any of them sick or dying? Did anyone need help? Neighbors and family could not even gather to console each other since everyone just stayed at home.

Only Papá José Inés ventured out daily into the village, calling out to primos and neighbors from outside, asking about the sick and distributing the cebollas. The kids felt like prisoners, like the princess Scheherazade in their mother's Arabian storybook. They spent two months shut in the house, except on days they got to play on the long portal. Every other day they heard the bells, which echoed up and down the valley.

Papá y Amadito descargaron el carro. De una vez, Anita y Mamá empezaron a hacer el jarabe de cebolla morada por si alguien lo necesitaba. Las cajas de cebollas se quedaron en el portal para que los vecinos las pudieran recoger sin tener que pasar para adentro. Colgando de la viga del techo había un saco de raíz de oshá fresca. No había nada más que hacer excepto esperar y rezar el rosario a la nochecita. Como no se podía hacer mucho contra la influenza, Amadito se sentía apenado y frustrado. Ahora ni podían salir a jugar, ni buscar a sus amigos. ¿Cuántos estarían enfermos o muertos? ¿Quiénes necesitarían ayuda? Los vecinos y la familia no podían juntarse para consolarse porque todo el mundo se encerraba en la casa.

Sólo Papá José Inés salía a diario a la placita, llamando a los primos y a los vecinos desde fuera, preguntando por los enfermos y distribuyendo las cebollas. Los muchitos se sentían como cautivos, como la princesa Scheherazade en el libro de cuentos árabes de su mamá. Pasaron dos meses encerrados en la casa, excepto cuando se les permitía jugar en el largo portal. Cada otro día escuchaban las campanas que esparcían su eco a lo largo del vallecito.

"Dios da y Dios quita . . . God giveth and He taketh away." Papá said with tears in his eyes when the bells tolled. Every night the family gave thanks to God for making it through another day. One morning Papá José Inés left for Taos to see if he could get any news. *La Revista de Taos* had stopped publishing for a month. The influenza had taken its editor, too.

Like a good mother, Mamá Virginia tried to turn all her worrying into action. She mobilized the kids to scrub down the house with *jabón de lejía*, lye soap. She was the captain of her little troops. The enemy was the disease that threatened her family and community from every side.

"What more can be done? What more can I do?" She wondered out loud.

She felt helpless faced with the influenza. When would there ever be an effective remedy for it? Some people were so desperate that they placed the purple onions—or any onions they could find— under the bed of the person sick with flu. How could they absorb the illness? It just didn't make sense. Other people made incense from bunches of *chamizo pardo* to bless the houses with smoke. Was it doing any good? Drinking the purple onion syrup or tea made of oshá or sage seemed more reasonable.

"Dios da y Dios quita," decía Papá con lágrimas en los ojos cuando doblaban las campanas. Cada noche la familia daba gracias a Dios por haber vivido otro día más. Una mañana Papá José Inés salió para Taos a buscar noticias. *La Revista de Taos* había dejado de publicarse por un mes. La influenza se había llevado al editor.

Como buena madre, Mamá Virginia intentó transformar todas sus ansias en acción. Movilizó a los niños para limpiar toda la casa con jabón de lejía. Era la capitana de su pequeña tropa. El enemigo era la enfermedad que amenazaba a su familia y a la comunidad desde todos lados.

"¿Qué más se puede hacer? ¿Qué más puedo yo hacer?" Pensaba en voz alta.

Se sentía inútil ante a la influenza. ¿Cuándo habrá un remedio efectivo? Había gente tan desesperada que ponían las cebollas moradas— o cualquier cebolla—debajo de la cama de la persona enferma. ¿Cómo pueden absorber el mal? No tenía sentido. Otra gente hacía incienso de las ramitas del chamizo pardo para bendecir las casas con humo. ¿Qué efecto podía tener esto? Por lo menos tomar el jarabe de la cebolla morada o el té de oshá o chamizo parecía más razonable.

"*Ojalá hubiera una vacuna para la influencia . . .* I wish there were a vaccine against the flu," she prayed. She remembered the miracle stories her elders had told her of la vacuna and how many people it saved from the deadly viruela. At least for the smallpox there was something effective she could do for her children. She got down the box with the family papers from the attic and found an envelope that she had carefully sealed and put away several years ago. Inside were three dried scabs from smallpox vaccinations she had done on herself and her first two children.

Even though la viruela was now rare in New Mexico, it still lurked in the shadows, ready to strike people down or scar them for life. She remembered an old spinster aunt from her childhood who had almost lost an eye to the scarring. Her eyelashes and eyebrows never did grow back. For the rest of her life, people unkindly nicknamed her *La Cacariza,* "Scarface." Mamá Virginia shuddered with the memory and returned to her project with new resolve. She had learned from her mother how long to soak the vaccination scabs, how to sterilize a penknife in a candle flame, how to clean the arm with alcohol, scratch a little cross on the skin, and rub the scab into the cut.

"*Ojalá hubiera una vacuna para la influencia,*" rezaba. Se acordaba de los milagros que contaban los viejitos de la vacuna y cuánta gente salvó de la terrible viruela. Por lo menos había algo efectivo que podía hacer para sus hijos. Bajó la cajita con los papeles de la familia del piso de arriba y sacó un sobre que había sellado cuidadosamente y guardado hacía años. Adentro había tres costras de vacunas que ella hizo para sí misma y para sus primeros dos hijos.

Aunque la viruela ya no era nada común en Nuevo México, todavía acechaba en las sombras, lista para tumbar a la gente o desfigurarla de por vida. Se acordaba de una tía solterona que conoció en su juventud que casi perdió un ojo por las cicatrices de la viruela. Nunca recuperó sus pestañas y sus cejas. Por el resto de su vida la gente cruelmente le decía "La Cacariza." Mamá Virginia tembló al recordarlo y volvió a su proyecto con nuevo empeño. Había aprendido de su madre cuánto tiempo remojar las costras, cómo esterilizar una navajita en la llama de una vela, cómo limpiar el brazo con alcohol, cómo picar una crucita en la piel, y frotar la costra sobre la pequeña herida.

While Anita distracted her brothers and sisters with games and dolls in another part of the house, Amadito helped his mother prepare for la vacuna. One by one, he brought Enrique, Isaac, Pablita, and little Fermilia into the kitchen and calmed them down.

"You must be brave like soldiers, *como niños héroes*," he told them, as his mother had.

Amadito's brothers sat still while Mamá Virginia made the cross, and she let Amadito rub in the scab. A piece of ribbon candy was the reward for bravery. While Mamá Virginia held her little girls tight to her breast, Amadito made the little crosses and finished the vaccinations. Only Fermilia cried.

Mientras Anita distraía sus hermanos con juegos y muñecas en otra parte de la casa, Amadito ayudó a su madre con las preparaciones para la vacuna. Uno por uno, trajo a Enrique, a Isaac, a Pablita y a la pequeña Fermilia a la cocina para calmarlos.

"Tienen que ser valientes como soldados, como niños héroes," les dijo, como su mamá les había dicho.

Los hermanos de Amadito se sentaron quietos mientras Mamá Virginia les hacía la crucita, y dejaba que Amadito les frotara la costra. Un pedazo de dulce de cinta fue el premio por la valentía. Mientras Mamá Virginia apretaba a sus hijitas contra su pecho, Amadito les hizo las crucitas y terminó las vacunas. Solamente Fermilia lloró.

That night when the younger kids were in bed, Mamá Virginia gathered Anita and Amadito together for a story. They had many questions about what had happened that day. How could the vaccination help them? If the mysterious viruela was so bad, how come the kids joked and sang about it? What did la vacuna have to do with *vacas*, with cows? Mamá Virginia told them how cows had saved people from la viruela by sharing their immunity, their protection from disease. What they shared was cowpox, their own disease that helped save people from the dreaded smallpox.

"Cows share their milk, even their meat to feed us. *Diosito* has given them this other talent so they can save our lives, too!" Mamá Virginia said.

"Mamá, *mañana* we will give a special treat of some apples to La Pinta." She was the family milk cow.

"*Mis hijos*, you are as kind as you are curious! Now I will tell you about your Nana María Peregrina, your great-grandmother, the bravest girl in Chamisal."

Esa noche cuando los pequeños estaban en la cama, Mamá Virginia juntó a Anita y Amadito para contarles un cuento. Tenían muchas preguntas sobre lo que había pasado ese día. ¿Cómo podían las vacunas ayudarles? Si la misteriosa viruela era tan malvada, ¿cómo es que los niños cantaban y se burlaban de ella? ¿Qué tenía la vacuna que ver con las vacas? Mamá Virginia les dijo cómo las vacas habían salvado a la gente de la viruela compartiendo su inmunidad, su protección de la enfermedad. Lo que compartían era la viruela de vacas, su propia enfermedad que ayudaba a la gente a protegerse de la viruela que mataba a la gente.

"Las vacas comparten su leche, hasta su carne para alimentarnos. ¡Diosito les ha dado este otro talento para que puedan salvarnos la vida también!" les dijo Mamá Virginia.

"Mamá, mañana daremos un regalito, unas manzanas a La Pinta." Ella era la vaca lechera de la familia.

"Mis hijos, ¡son tan buenos como curiosos! Ahora les voy a contar de su Nana María Peregrina, su tatarabuela, la muchacha más valiente de Chamisal."

She told them stories from the days of the *antepasados*, our ancestors, about the Niños Héroes, those valiant children who brought the blessings of la vacuna to New Mexico. Mamá Virginia had heard about the Niños growing up and in school had read about Doctor Larrañaga, the army surgeon from Santa Fe. Long, long ago, in the fall of 1804, he recruited eight boys, sons of the soldiers from the Presidio fort, to travel down the Camino Real to Chihuahua to bring back la vacuna the following spring of 1805. They would get it from La Real Expedición Filantrópica de la Vacuna, the royal expedition that was traveling north by coach with the famous Doctor Balmis from Spain to vaccinate all the people of New Spain.

In those earliest years of the nineteenth century, the surest way to transport the vaccine was in the bodies of healthy, robust children. When the little cross was scratched on their arms, they were vaccinated with fluid from the blister of the previous child. Then, ten days later a new blister would form in the same spot. The serum from one blister could vaccinate dozens and dozens of people if the expedition was in a settlement or the next child carrier if they were still traveling. The children were vaccinated in pairs to ensure that the vaccine would not be lost.

Les contó historias de los tiempos de los antepasados, nuestros antepasados, sobre los Niños Héroes, aquellos valientes jóvenes que trajeron la bendición de la vacuna a Nuevo México. Mamá Virginia había oído de estos niños cuando crecía, y en la escuela leyó sobre el Doctor Larrañaga, el cirujano militar de Santa Fe. Hace muchísimo tiempo, en el otoño de 1804, el doctor reclutó a ocho niños, hijos de los soldados del Presidio, y viajó con ellos por el Camino Real a Chihuahua para traer la vacuna a Santa Fe la siguiente primavera de 1805. La tomaron de La Real Expedición Filantrópica de la Vacuna, que viajaba al norte por coche con el famoso Doctor Balmis de España para vacunar a toda la gente de la Nueva España.

En esos primeros años del siglo diecinueve, la manera más segura de transportar la vacuna era en los cuerpos de niños saludables y robustos. Se les rascaban las crucitas en los brazos, y se les vacunaba con el suero de la ampolla del niño anterior. Así, de ese modo, diez días después, se les formaba una nueva ampollita en el mismo lugar. El suero de una ampolla podía vacunar a docenas y docenas de personas, si la expedición se encontraba en una población, o al próximo niño, si todavía andaban viajando. Los niños fueron vacunados en parejas para asegurar que no se perdiera la vacuna.

"When the Niños Héroes arrived in each town, they put on their *tricornios*, their three cornered hats. They each dressed up in a yellow suit with a red sash," said Mamá Virginia. "They were treated to banquets, the best food and sweets that each town had. The people knew that their health depended on them."

The story continued well past bedtime. But Anita and Amadito listened in amazement. They learned how la vacuna could be lost, how the chain of transmission from child to child could be broken. The first time this happened, Doctor Larrañaga's helpers visited all the ranches they could until they found a milk cow sick with cowpox blisters. The next time it was lost a couple of years later, another epidemic was on the way and an emergency package was rushed from Chihuahua with special instructions for a new technique. Inside was an envelope with dried scabs from vaccinations. They were to be ground and mixed into a paste with drops of clean water, then rubbed onto the broken skin of the little cross. In that way the vaccine was revived and the campaign renewed.

"Cuando los Niños Héroes llegaban a cada placita se ponían sus tricornios. Cada uno se vestía con un traje amarillo con una banda colorada," contaba Mamá Virginia. "Les ofrecían un banquete, con la mejor comida y dulces que cada pueblo tenía. La gente entendía que su salud dependía de ellos."

La madre siguió con la historia más allá de la hora de acostarse. Pero Anita y Amadito escuchaban absortos. Aprendieron cómo la vacuna se podía perder, como la cadena de transmisión de niño en niño podría ser quebrada. La primera vez que pasó, los ayudantes del Doctor Larrañaga visitaron todos los ranchos que podían hasta que encontraron una vaca de leche enferma con la viruela de vacas. La próxima vez que se perdió fue algunos años más tarde. Se acercaba una epidemia y mandaron un paquete de emergencia desde Chihuahua con instrucciones especiales para una nueva técnica. Adentro había un sobre con costras secas de otras vacunas. Tenían que molerlas y mezclarlas con gotas de agua pura para hacer una pasta. Después frotaban la pasta en la cruz que picaban en la piel. Así revivieron la vacuna y la campaña se renovó.

"The same way we did our vaccinations!" Amadito shouted.

"This is when our María Peregrina became one of the Niños Héroes," Mamá Virginia added. "She was a little girl from Socorro whose parents had died in a flood. Like other orphans, she was recruited to help with la vacuna."

Amadito and Anita knew that their great-grandmother had been adopted, but this was the first they had heard of the rest of her story. In 1810, when she was nine years old, Doctor Larrañaga took Nana Peregrina to Santa Cruz de la Cañada. On a bright October day, the people had been called to the yard of the *convento* where the vaccinations were being drawn from her own blister. Two persons vaccinated that day were a young man and his sister from Chamisal. Their wagon was loaded with oats and beans that they brought to trade for corn, melons, and chile, which grow better down in the valley.

"That's right," said Amadito. "It's warmer! That's the same reason we trade down in Embudo. *Pero ¿qué pasó?* What happened to Nana Peregrina then?"

"¡Así hicimos nuestras vacunas" gritó Amadito!

"Fue en aquella campaña cuando nuestra María Peregrina se hizo uno de los Niños Héroes," añadió Mamá Virginia. "Ella era una muchita de Socorro y sus padres habían muerto en un diluvio. Como otros huérfanos, ella fue reclutada para ayudar con la vacuna."

Amadito y Anita sabía que su tatarabuela había sido adoptada, pero esta fue la primera vez que oyeron el resto de su historia. En 1810, cuando tenía nueve años, Nana Peregrina fue llevada a Santa Cruz de la Cañada por el Doctor Larrañaga. En un brillante día de octubre, la gente fue llamada al patio del convento donde estaban haciendo las vacunas de su propia ampollita. Dos personas vacunadas ese día fueron un joven y su hermana de Chamisal. Su carro estaba lleno de avena y frijoles que ellos habían llevado para cambiar para maíz, melones y chile, que crecen mejor en el valle.

"Es verdad," dijo Amadito. "¡Es más caliente! Por la misma razón vamos a cambalachear en Embudo. Pero, ¿qué pasó? ¿Qué le pasó a Nana Peregrina después?"

"Her duty was done as soon as her arm healed. She played her part to distribute la vacuna. Since she was an orphan, she was invited to Chamisal, where she gave the vaccination to everyone who needed it. The viruela swept through again, but nobody died. She was adopted and married into our family when she was a young woman. Her blood is in your veins, and her spirit is with you!"

The next day Papá José Inés returned with good news. Their primos in Taos were in good health. People were getting better. Mamá Virginia explained how she decided to vaccinate the children, just in case, and how helpful the oldest children had been, especially Amadito.

"Ese muchito nació para curar . . . that kid was born to help cure people," Papá Inés said proudly. *"Tiene buen corazón . . .* he has a good heart. Someday he will become a *médico."* He knew it would come to pass.

"Una vez que su brazo se sanó, su misión quedó cumplida. Hizo su contribución en la distribución de la vacuna. Como era huérfana, le invitaron a Chamisal, donde vacunó a toda la gente que la necesitaba. La viruela vino una vez más, pero nadie murió. Ella fue adoptada y se casó con uno de nuestra familia cuando era joven. ¡Su sangre está en las venas de ustedes, y su espíritu los acompaña!"

El próximo día Papá José Inés regresó con buenas nuevas. Los primos de Taos estaban en buena salud. La gente se mejoraba. Mamá Virginia le explicó como decidió vacunar a los muchitos, por si acaso, y lo mucho que le había ayudados los mayorcitos, especialmente Amadito.

"Ese muchito nació para curar," Papá Inés dijo con mucho orgullo. "Tiene buen corazón. Algún día será médico." Sabía que iba a pasar.

The story of Nana María Peregrina was an inspiration to all, especially in a time of epidemic and death. Children play such a special part in the health of their families!

In the next weeks, the influenza subsided in Chamisal. By Christmas 1918, Taos County was in recovery. The black hand of Death was loosening its grip, but the death toll was high. *Gracias a Dios*, nobody in the Domínguez family got sick or died, but they did lose four primos and many friends. Chamisal, a village of several hundred, lost over forty people. A thousand died throughout all New Mexico.

"*Sólo Diosito sabe cuántos* . . . only the Good Lord knows how many," all the people would say.

It would take a generation for the people of New Mexico, the nation, and the world to recover from the tragic pandemic of the influenza. But Nuevo Mexicanos had survived many hardships and perils in their four-hundred-year history in this land. We remember the strength of our antepasados and all those that came before— their ingenuity and their sacrifice. They claimed the future as their own. We are all the children of the Niños Héroes.

La historia de Nana María Peregrina fue una inspiración para todos, especialmente en los tiempos de epidemias y muerte. ¡Los niños jugaron un papel muy especial en la salud de sus familias!

En las próximas semanas, la influenza estaba menguando en Chamisal. Para la Navidad de 1918, el condado de Taos estaba recuperándose. La mano negra de la Muerte aflojó, pero se había llevado a muchos. Gracias a Dios, nadie en la familia Domínguez se enfermó ni murió, pero perdieron a cuatro primos y a muchos amigos. Chamisal, una placita de varios cientos de habitantes, perdió a más de cuarenta. Mil personas murieron en todo Nuevo México.

"Sólo Diosito sabe cuántos," todo el mundo decía.

Tomaría una generación para que la gente de Nuevo México, la nación y el mundo se recuperara de la trágica pandemia de la influenza. Pero los nuevomexicanos ya habían sobrevivido tiempos difíciles y los peligros de una historia de cuatro cientos años en esta tierra. Recordamos la fortaleza de nuestros antepasados y toda la gente de antes—su resolución y su sacrificio. Ellos hicieron suyo el futuro. Todos somos los hijos de los Niños Héroes.

EPILOGUE AND BIOGRAPHICAL NOTE

Before the ordeal of the 1918 influenza epidemic, the family of José Inés Domínguez and Virginia Rodríguez of Chamisal and Guadalupita, New Mexico, had already lost two babies to diphtheria, which hit rural communities hard almost every winter. Two new children were born and named with their names. After 1918, Carmen and Jorge were born. The youngest child, Jorge, was stricken with meningitis but happily survived. All his seven brothers and sisters—Anita, José Amado, Enrique, Isaac, Pablita, Fermilia, and Carmen—got their educations and enjoyed professional careers. Papá José Inés dry-farmed pinto beans and worked in the mines of Colorado to get them through school. Three of the Domínguez children became teachers like their mother. Born in 1909, José Amado Domínguez became the first Nuevo Mexicano physician in Taos County. He graduated from Kirksville College of Osteopathic Medicine in Missouri and served his innumerable patients for fifty years until his own death in 1999. He was the last doctor to make house calls to the villages of northern New Mexico where he grew up.

The twentieth-century part of this story is true. The nineteenth-century adventures of Nana María Peregrina are historical fiction, although her name is in the family, and she is an ancestor.

Peace and good health!

EPÍLOGO Y NOTA BIOGRÁFICA

Antes del desafío de la epidemia de la influenza de 1918, la familia de José Inés Domínguez y Virginia Rodríguez de Chamisal y Guadalupita, Nuevo México, ya había perdido dos bebés a causa de la difteria, que pegaba en las comunidades rurales casi todos los inviernos. Luego tuvieron dos nuevos hijos que fueron bautizados con los mismos nombres de los fallecidos. Después de 1918 nacieron Carmen y Jorge. El hijo menor, Jorge, sufrió la meningitis pero felizmente recuperó. Todos sus siete hermanos—Anita, José Amado, Enrique, Isaac, Pablita, Fermilia y Carmen—se educaron y tuvieron carreras profesionales. Papá José Inés cultivó frijoles pintos al temporal y trabajó en las minas de Colorado para educarlos. Tres de los niños se hicieron maestros como su madre. Nacido en 1909, José Amado Domínguez fue el primer médico nuevomexicano en el condado de Taos. Se graduó de Kirksville College of Osteopathic Medicine en Missouri y sirvió a sus innumerables pacientes por cincuenta años hasta su propia muerte en 1999. Fue el último doctor que hacía visitas de casa en las placitas del norte de Nuevo México donde creció.

La parte de esta historia del siglo veinte es verídica. Las aventuras de Nana María Peregrina son ficción histórica, aunque su nombre perteneció a una antepasada de la misma familia.

¡Paz y salud!

Global Pandemics and *Remedios Nuevomexicanos*

Michael León Trujillo

At first glance, global epidemics of influenza and smallpox may seem difficult or even callous subjects for a children's book. But in *Amadito and the Hero Children*, they fuel an amazing story appropriate and inspiring for children and adults alike. It should not be a surprise that a professor of New Mexico folklore would pick such subject matter. As the collective wisdom and practice of the people, folklore often confronts real world struggles and imbues them with meaning. Children have long told and retold stories of hope and pain. Through their eyes complex concepts become accessible. In this tale, and like the folklore that Enrique Lamadrid has long written about and taught, culture, history, mortality, and hope are woven together into a life-affirming tale. *Amadito* is the story of how a boy and his family in a seemingly isolated mountain valley of New Mexico confronted global smallpox and influenza epidemics in the nineteenth and twentieth centuries, utilized techniques brought from distant lands and passed down by their ancestors, and changed the world for the better.

Disease and epidemics, the pain and struggle they bring, as well as the meaning and hope fostered in such struggles have long been part of the human experience. In the aftermath of the 1492 Columbian Encounter, agricultural, technological, and cultural exchanges changed the world. But the transfer of disease had immediate and catastrophic consequences. Millions of Native Americans died of diseases for which they had no immunity. As resistance developed in the natives and *mestizos*, epidemics continued to ravage the Americas. Lamadrid reveals in this book's final sentences that the twentieth century events represented in the text really happened and the nineteenth century events are historical fiction. For young readers, the story renders events, news stories, family history, and their own challenges understandable. For teachers and parents, *Amadito* speaks to abstract but urgent matters such as globalization, while a family story illustrates the importance of local history and struggle.

Local History / Local Knowledge

Amadito and the Hero Children expresses the rich layers of local New Mexico history and culture. It depicts real events in the Taos County village of Chamisal, for the book's main protagonist, Amadito, was a real child. Details in the story, such as the pinto bean harvest and Amadito's trip with his father from Chamisal to Dixon and the Embudo station are true, but the story lines recount both history and fiction. Lamadrid describes events that span nearly two hundred years and New Mexico's transition from Spanish to Mexican to American government. In the fall of 1918 during the U.S. period, the child Amadito and his community endure the global flu epidemic that killed millions of people worldwide. In the fall of 1810 during the final years of Spanish colonial rule, a fictional nine-year-old orphan from central New Mexico, María Peregrina, carries the smallpox vaccine from the town of Santa Cruz de la Cañada to the village of Chamisal. She accompanies the real Santa Fe physician, Dr. Cristóval Larrañaga, who in 1805 brought the real children who transported the vaccine from Mexico's interior

Amadito at age sixteen. Menaul School football team, Albuquerque.

to the ranches and towns of New Mexico, the far northern frontier of New Spain. The scientific techniques he taught the people of New Mexico became home remedies. In this book's final pages we learn that the María Peregrina is an ancestor of Amadito, who grows up to be the real Dr. José Amado Domínguez, Taos County's first Nuevo Mexicano physician.

Mamá Virginia and Papá José Inés on their wedding day, 1908.

Lamadrid imbues this story with the richness of New Mexico's oral histories and knowledge often passed down through word of mouth rather than by historians. Nuevo Mexicano Spanish figures large in the book, with its mix of both standard and local terms for illnesses like *viruela* (smallpox), *sarampión* (measles), and *resfrío* (cold). The local term for the influenza epidemic of 1918 is *la influencia,* which sounds like "the influence," but is actually a phonological adaptation of the Italian loan word *influenza.* Interestingly, influenza also means "influence" in Italian, in reference to the ancient belief that catastrophic outbreaks of disease were caused by the influence, literally the "in-flow" or emanations, of certain bad stars. At the center of the story is a rhyme, "Frijolitos pintos," one of the most popular and recognizable Nuevo Mexicano children's songs. On the surface it seems to be nonsensical, but in the opening scene of the story, Amadito begins to suspect its deeper meaning. The song mitigates and even pokes fun at the diseases that swept New Mexico and the terrible scars they left on survivors:

Primero da viruela,	First smallpox strikes,
luego sarampión,	then the measles,
le quedó la cara	his/her face was left
como un chicarrón.	like a pork crackling.

As they acquired the English language, Nuevo Mexicano children would soon learn another nonsense song and game that recalls another pandemic that decimated the population of Europe in the Middle Ages, the Black Plague:

Ring around the rosie,
pocket full of posies.
Ashes, ashes,
we all fall down. . . .

The first symptoms were swelling of lymph nodes and spot rashes or "rosies" that swelled into "buboes" and erupted. The only remedies were the "posies" or herbs, since it took centuries to discover the real causes and carriers of the plague—infected fleas. Death came within days. Ashes to ashes.

Although the pharmacopeia of herbal remedies in New Mexico is rich and powerful, there was little protection against smallpox before the vaccine. The only potential *remedios* or remedies against the flu were *oshá* (wild celery root), the tea and the incense blessings from *chamizo pardo* (gray sage), and the syrupy mixture of *cebolla morada* (purple onion) and *piloncillo* (raw sugar cones). Prayers and blessings were a reassuring spiritual recourse. In the story, Amadito's father is desperate to protect his young son from the flu and gives him a culturally hybrid blessing: the traditional Catholic invocation of God's power plus a Native American smoke purification. He asks the boy to walk through puffs of cedar smoke three times as he says, *"En el nombre del Padre, del Hijo, del Espíritu Santo . . .* In the name of the Father, the Son, the Holy Spirit."

Global Circulations: Influenza and Variola

Amadito is rich with local history and culture, but it also connects to regional, national, and transnational circulations. Distant events and their repercussions in distant locations may be mapped through the transmission of contagions across the globe. The deadliest of all were influenza and smallpox. From the remote village of Chamisal, the "globalization" of disease is specifically addressed in our story. Epidemics with global reach are termed pandemics and are linked to regional, national, and global networks or systems of trade and colonization. The enormous expansion of Spanish and Portuguese colonization in the sixteenth century and British, French, and Dutch colonization in the eighteenth and nineteenth centuries transmitted diseases from the so-called Old World to the New World and between colonial centers and remote frontiers. Diseases often arrived before the first face-to-face contacts between natives and explorers. In at least one case in North America, smallpox was used as a biological weapon: in the 1763 siege of Fort Pitt (now Pittsburgh, Pennsylvania) when officers of the English Army gave infected blankets to their Indian enemies. In the Spanish colonies, the smallpox epidemics that regularly devastated the population were of great concern to civil and religious authorities. Even the story of the American colonists' revolt against England may be persuasively told against the backdrop of the spread and toll of disease.

In the twentieth century, the 1918 influenza pandemic that raged around the globe and took the lives of millions of people can only be understood in the context of World War I. In Chamisal, Amadito's mother, Virginia Domínguez, reads real news from *La Revista de Taos*, the real newspaper that reports the deaths in France of four soldiers from Taos and Río Arriba counties from the flu rather than from German shells. Within days, the epidemic penetrated the valleys of northern New Mexico. The only effective defense to ward off the flu was the *cuarentena*, or quarantine, learned during Spanish colonial era epidemics. As the claustrophobia set in, Mamá Virginia became more desperate to protect her children. Since she was powerless against the flu, she decided to do something within her power, to vaccinate her

children against la viruela, with the help of her son. After all, the last outbreak of smallpox had been in one of the Indian Pueblos in 1899, well within living memory. Her home remedy was also the pride of nineteenth-century science. Smallpox was not eliminated in the United States until the late 1940s or in Mexico until the early 1950s. These resolute efforts by Amadito's family and neighbors provide the hope in the story. They are also the place where the specificity of local history and global circulations meet.

Domínguez family home and store. Chamisal, NM, ca. 1918.

Deadly and Benign Inoculations: Variolation and Vaccine

In northern New Mexico, children and parents confronted illness and found healing in vaccines originally brought in the bodies of children. Formal medical knowledge from faraway places became the local knowledge of Nuevo Mexicano ancestors. Here we recall the real story of the hero children from Santa Fe, the Niños Héroes as they were called in their own time, who carried the smallpox vaccine north from Chihuahua to New Mexico. Their story demonstrates that it is not only death that travels across oceans and along the old Camino Real, but deliverance. Medical knowledge and technology sanctioned by the centers of power followed the same paths as colonization and disease. With historical fiction Lamadrid links the Hero Children to Amadito through María Peregrina.

In colonial Mexico, public authorities used the risky techniques of variolation as a defense against the imminent threat of smallpox (*variola* in Latin). Variolation was the inoculation or introduction into the body of scrapings from the blisters of smallpox victims through a scratch on the skin or sniffing the dried powder. A healthy person would then contract a less virulent smallpox infection. Vaccination is an inoculation from the sores of the cowpox (*vaccinia* in Latin), a related but nonfatal disease. *Vaca* is, of course, *cow* in Spanish. The technique of vaccination was pioneered by English physician Edward Jenner, who almost died from being variolated as a child.

Because of the terrible smallpox epidemics in Spain's colonial possessions, an expedition was sent by Spain's King Charles IV under the leadership of Dr. Francisco Xavier de Balmis to distribute the benign and effective smallpox vaccine throughout its colonial possessions. The Expedición Real Filantrópica de la Vacuna, or Royal Philanthropic Expedition of the Vaccine, set sail on November 30, 1803, from La Coruña, Spain, in the twilight years of the vast Spanish empire. It was

Cristóval María Larrañaga, report of children vaccinated, May 24, 1805. Spanish Archives of New Mexico, Series II, 1621–1821, Roll 15, Frame 639, Twitchell #1833. Courtesy New Mexico State Records Center and Archives.

the earliest and most ambitious public health project in modern times. In addition to the live vaccine, the expedition brought Balmis's own Spanish translation of the French physician Jacques-Louis Moreau de la Sarthe's treatise on vaccination, *Tratado histórico y práctio de la vacuna* (Moreau de la Sarthe 1803). Balmis and his collaborators visited the Canary Islands, Puerto Rico, Cuba, Venezuela, Colombia, Ecuador, Peru, Mexico, the Philippines, and China, vaccinating more than 100,000 people in Spanish colonies, including 45,000 people in Mexico alone.

The Balmis expedition began with twenty children from La Coruña's orphanage, who would be the most secure carriers of the vaccine. The king himself adopted them to make sure they would find proper homes after their work was done. The Niños Héroes from Santa Fe, who would carry the vaccine from Chihuahua, were recruited from the families of soldiers of the Presidio de Santa Fe by Dr. Cristóval Larrañaga, the Basque physician also stationed there. Lamadrid describes the process of vaccination in the story:

> In those earliest years of the nineteenth century, the surest way to transport the vaccine was in the bodies of healthy, robust children. When the little cross was scratched on their arms, they were vaccinated with fluid from the blister of the previous child. Then, ten days later a new blister would form in the same spot. The serum from one blister could vaccinate dozens and dozens of people if the expedition was in a settlement or the next child carrier if they were still traveling.

Not revealed in Lamadrid's text is the fact that inoculation by variolation and vaccination were controversial topics in eighteenth- and nineteenth-century medicine. Many people became sick and died from variolations, although a much smaller percentage than those that contracted the disease through "natural" means. People naturally mistrusted the vaccine as well. The children who brought protection to the peoples of the Spanish empire did so at great personal risk and were real heroes in every sense of the word.

After his arrival in Santa Fe on May 24, 1805, Dr. Larrañaga worked selflessly and tirelessly for years to spread the vaccine across New Mexico and teach the people how to use it. The fictional María Peregrina joins him on one of his trips to Santa Cruz de la Cañada and continues north to Chamisal. These heroic children of the twilight era of Spanish colonial rule are, in Lamadrid's story, the inspiration for American-era Amadito to travel east to Missouri to earn his degree at the Kirksville College of Osteopathic Medicine. We are not told that Amadito will also become Lamadrid's father-in-law, but that is also a key part of the story. In this way, Lamadrid draws a line of continuity from the children who migrated to and from Mexico's interior, to María Peregrina's pilgrimage to what would become Taos County, to Amadito, and to Dr. José Amado Domínguez and his own children and grandchildren. All are participants in global circulations fraught with both danger and healing. As the H1N1 pandemic of 2009 shows, global circulations continue to manifest themselves in the form of contagions. This book actually began as the "2009 Flu Plan" that Lamadrid was asked to write in his professional role as chair of the Department of Spanish and Portuguese at the University of New Mexico. There is much work yet to be done, and we hope that the generation of Amadito's great-grandchildren will find similar inspiration.

Dr. Larrañaga's signature and rubric. Detail from letter on page 54.

FURTHER READINGS

Aldrete, J. Antonio
2004 "Smallpox Vaccination in the Early 19th Century Using Live Carriers: The Travels of Francisco Xavier de Balmis." *Southern Medical Journal* 97 (4): 375–78.

Austin Alchón, Suzanne
2003 *A Pest in the Land: New World Epidemics in a Global Perspective.* Albuquerque: University of New Mexico Press.

Baca, Oswald G.
2000 "Infectious Diseases and Smallpox Politics in New Mexico's Río Abajo, 1847–1920." *New Mexico Historical Review* 75: 107–27.

Crosby, Alfred W., Jr.
2003 *America's Forgotten Pandemic: The Influenza of 1918,* 2nd edition. New York: Cambridge University Press.
1972 *The Columbian Exchange: Biological and Cultural Consequences of 1492.* Westport, Conn.: Greenwood Press.

Díaz de Yraola, Gonzalo
2003 *The Spanish Royal Philanthropic Expedition: The Round-the-World Voyage of the Smallpox Vaccine, 1803–1810.* Trans. Catherine Mark. Madrid: Instituto de Historia, Consejo Superior de Investigaciones Científicas.

Fenn, Elizabeth A.
2002 *Pox Americana: The Great Smallpox Epidemic of 1775–82.* New York: Hill and Wang.

Frost, Richard H.
1990 "The Pueblo Indian Smallpox Epidemic in New Mexico, 1898–1899." *Bulletin of the History of Medicine* 64 (3): 417–45.

McCaa, Robert
1998 "Inoculation: An Easy Means of Protecting People or Propagating Smallpox? Spain, New Spain, and Chiapas, 1779–1800." *Boletín Mexicana de Historia y Filosofía de la Medicina* 2, nueva época (septiembre 1998): 4–11.

Melzer, Richard
1982 "A Dark and Terrible Moment: The Spanish Flu Epidemic of 1918 in New Mexico." *New Mexico Historical Review* 57 (3): 216.

Mignolo, Walter D.
2000 *Local Histories / Global Designs.* Princeton, N.J.: Princeton University Press.

Moreau de la Sarthe, Jacques-Louis
1803 *Tratado histórico y práctico de la vacuna.* Trans. Francisco Xavier de Balmis. Madrid: Imprenta Real.

Pearcy, Thomas L.
1990 "The Control of Smallpox in New Spain's Northern Borderlands." *Journal of the West* 29 (3): 90–98.

Pettit, Dorothy A.
2008 *A Cruel Wind: Pandemic Flu in America, 1918–1920.* Murf, Tenn.: Timberlane Books.

Rees, Clifford M.
2005 "Spanish Influenza in New Mexico, 1918–1919: The Role of the State and Local Public Health Measures." *ABA Health eSource* 2, 4 (December).

Simmons, Marc
1966 "New Mexico's Smallpox Epidemics of 1780–1781." *New Mexico Historical Review* 41 (4): 319–26.

GLOSSARY

Amado [**Amadito**]: beloved [name]

antepasados: ancestors

buena/o: good

cacariza/o: scarface

Camino Real: Royal Road

camposanto: holy ground, graveyard

cara: face

cebolla: onion

chamisa: sage brush

Chamisal: field of sage brush [place name]

chamizo pardo: gray sage brush

chicharrón: pork crackling

claveles: carnations

convento: convent

cotencio: tarp

cuántos: how many

cuarantena: quarantine

cuestecita: little summit or hill

curandero: curer

dar [*da*]: to give

Dios, Diosito: God, little/dear God

"*Dios da y Dios quita*": "God giveth and God taketh away" [saying]

"*En el nombre del Padre, del Hijo, del Espíritu Santo*": "In the name of the Father, the Son, and Holy Spirit" [blessing]

Embudo: funnel [place name]

en: in

enamorados: sweethearts

enterrar [*enterrando*]: to bury

entrar [*entra*]: enter

española: Spanish

Española: Spanish woman [place name]

estar [*está*]: to be

frijolitos pintos: little pinto beans

"*Gracias a Dios*": "Thanks be to God" [saying]

gratis: free

guangoche: gunny sack

guardar [*guarde*]: to keep or guard

haber [*hubiera*]: to be

héroes: heroes

hija/o: daughter, son

influenza, "*influencia*": flu

jabón de lejía: lye soap

Jicarita: little gourd [place name]

mañana: tomorrow

María Peregrina: Mary the pilgrim [name]

mi'jito: my little son [contraction]

morado: purple

morir: to die

muchacha/o: girl, boy

muchita/o: little girl, little boy

nacer [**nació**]: to be born

nana: grandmother

niño/a: child

nuevomexicanos: New Mexicans

ojalá: may god grant

oshá: porters lovage [medicinal root]

para: for

Peñasco: boulder [place name]

pepenar: to pick

pero: but

piloncillo: raw sugar cones

pinta/o: painted

¿por qué?: why?

portal: porch

primero: first

primo: cousin

puela: frying pan

pulmonía: pneumonia

quedar [**quedó**]: to remain

¿qué pasó?: what happened?

La Real Expedición Filantrópica de la Vacuna: Royal Philanthropic Expedition of the Vaccine

resfriado: cold

revista: review or magazine

rosario: the rosary

saber [**sabe, sé**]: to know

salarata: baking soda

sarampión: measles

seguir [**sigan**]: continue

Sierra de la Sangre de Cristo: Mountains of the Blood of Christ [place name]

sólo: only

sufrir [**sufren**]: to suffer

tiempo: time

trilla: threshing

vaca: cow

vacuna: vaccine

varicela: chicken pox

velorio: wake

vida: life

viga: roof beam

viruela: smallpox